GW00857412

THE

DINOSAUR

IN THE

SHED

STEPHEN HUGHES
ILLUSTRATED BY EMILY POOL

Matador
9 Priory Business Park,
Wistow Road, Kibworth Beauchamp,
Leicestershire. LE8 0RX
Tel: 0116 279 2299
Email: books@troubador.co.uk
Web: www.troubador.co.uk/matador
Twitter: @matadorbooks

ISBN 978 1788035 170

British Library Cataloguing in Publication Data.
A catalogue record for this book is available from the British Library.

Typeset in 13pt Century Schoolbook by Troubador Publishing Ltd, Leicester, UK

Matador is an imprint of Troubador Publishing Ltd

Stephen: For Hannah, Harry and Louise.

Emily: For my family.

Chapter 1

The Dinosaur in the Shed

Harry the Dinosaur lives in our shed
With a colour TV and a nice comfy bed,
Flowery curtains, a torch for a light
And a big squidgy ted that he cuddles at
night.

The story of how he came to stay
Starts on a cold and blustery day.

We were out for a walk, my mum, dad and me
When we found this big egg sitting under a
tree.
We carefully carried it home from the park
And found a good place that was safe, warm
and dark.

Each day I'd go to the cupboard and
undo the catch
Looking for signs that the egg would
soon hatch.
I knew it had happened when one
day I heard,
"I don't know what it is… but it isn't
a bird."

As dinosaurs went he wasn't enormous,
Nowhere as big as a tyrannosaurus.
But life in the house got harder and harder
When he ate all the food in the fridge and the larder.

He lay on the table and buckled the legs,
He played with Mum's washing and chewed
all her pegs,
He tripped over the cat and stood on Dad's feet,
When he sat on the sofa he took up two seats.

He bumped and he banged when he walked
through a door
And knocked over a vase which went crash on
the floor.
If he turned round too quickly then quite
without fail
He'd break something else with his long
waggy tail.
When the dog wasn't looking he'd eat all his
food
Which put the poor dog in a terrible mood.
Harry was gentle, just like a mouse,
Just too big and clumsy to live in a house.

"I'm sorry," said Dad, "I know Harry's a friend
But he'll just get too big for the house in the end."
And just at that moment I had a bad feeling
As a dinosaur's bottom appeared through the
ceiling.
And then an idea popped into my head.
"Dad, why can't Harry go and live in the
shed?"

So later that evening we took Harry down
Dressed in Mum's floppy hat and Dad's
dressing gown.
A big woolly scarf pulled up to his eyes
Was the last crucial piece of Harry's disguise.
And to help get him settled Mum let him take
A bowl of hot chocolate and a whole ginger
cake.
With a push and a shove he was soon out of
sight
And I gave him a
cuddle and told
him, "Sleep
tight."

I went back to the house and climbed into bed
And knew we had many adventures ahead.
He'd grown out of the house so what would we
do
If in a few weeks he outgrew the shed too?
And if anyone saw him, and told what they
knew,
Would Harry be taken away to the zoo?
But for now, I thought, who could want more
Than to be best friends with a dinosaur?

Chapter 2

Harry in Danger

Mr Riley lives next door
I've never met someone so grumpy before
I've never ever seen him smile
You'd have more fun with a crocodile

Mr Riley doesn't like noise
He doesn't like girls and he doesn't like boys
Fun and games? He doesn't approve
He doesn't like us and he wishes we'd move
If I kick my ball over his fence
He'll say, "Silly girl, have you got no sense?"
He hasn't got friends, he never goes out
He often gets cross and likes a good shout
And he definitely didn't like what he saw
One day when I forgot to shut the shed door.

One Saturday morning I lay in bed
With the covers pulled up over my head.
"Get up now, please," I heard Mum yell
As someone rang the front doorbell.
Then she called to Dad, "Can you come down
dear?
Quickly now, there's a policeman here."

I heard the policeman clear his throat
And start to read the notes he'd wrote.
"A Mr Riley came to the station
And reported a worrying situation
That the previous day at half past four
He's sure he saw a dinosaur.
Oh and one more thing, I beg your pardon,
I forgot to say it was in your back garden."

"What!" said Dad with a nervous laugh.
"I'd be far more likely to have a giraffe.
I think I can ease my neighbours' fears,
There's been no dinosaurs here for quite a few
years."

"All the same," said the policeman," I must go and see.
Kindly show me the shed and please bring the key."
None of us had much to say
As nervously we made our way.
The door was slowly opened wide
Allowing the policeman to step inside.
In the corner Harry stood
So still, like he'd been carved from wood.
Clever thing, he'd seen the stranger
And quickly understood the danger.

"I'm sorry," said Dad, "I feel such a fool.
It's a model I made when I was at school."
The policeman stepped forward quite slowly
and then
Poked Harry hard with the end of his pen.
We all held our breath, our hearts beating
fast.
Had the truth about Harry been found out at
last?
Then swinging down on a silver thread,
A spider landed on Harry's head.
I gave Dad a nudge and we both froze
As it crawled down his face and straight up
his nose!

Harry stood still and didn't flinch,
No, he didn't move a single inch.
The policeman now was very near.
He looked in his eyes and inspected an ear,
He ran a finger round his jaw
And felt the sharpness of his claw.

"Well, well, wonders will never cease,
This really is a masterpiece.
It shouldn't be in here shut away,
You should put it on display."
And with that he made a final note,
Did up the buttons on his coat
And said, "I suppose before I go
I'd better let your neighbour know."

"Goodbye," said Dad. "Have a good day.
Call in if you're ever passing this way."
Then above the sound of the buzzing bees
We heard an enormous, explosive, SNEEZE!

The policeman turned and looked and said,
"That came from the direction of the shed."
"No," said Mum, "that's our neighbour, Jack.
Sounds like his hay fever's coming back."
"Poor soul," said the policeman, "I suffer from
that"
As he straightened his hair and pulled on his
hat.
And the last thing he said as he turned on his
heel
Was, "I still can't believe it, I thought it was
real."

We blew out our cheeks and all of us sighed
Then arms round each other we went inside.
Meanwhile with the danger past
Harry was able to move at last.
But next door, though the policeman had
tried,
Mr Riley wasn't satisfied.
He stared into the garden and shook his head.
He knew exactly what was in that shed.

Chapter 3

Harry Finds a Friend

In most people's sheds there are all sorts of things,
Like paint pots and tools and the odd ball of string,
Lawn mowers, bikes and an old washing line.
Well, I've got a dinosaur living in mine.

And I've got to say that he seemed happy enough,
Well, once we'd moved out all the cluttery stuff.
We always made sure he had plenty to eat
With a giant ice cream now and then as a treat.

But it wasn't enough and we should have
known
That he would get lonely and bored on his
own.
Harry was just like a puppy you see,
And happiest when he had company.

We knew that something had to be done,
That Harry needed urgent fun,
When one Saturday, about half past two,
During a family barbecue,
Dad said, "I may have made a mistake
But I'm sure the shed just started to shake."
He gave me a burger and said with a sigh,
"I'd better go and find out why."
He wasn't gone for very long
And I could see by his face there was

something wrong.
"You'll never guess
what I've just seen,
Harry's using his
bed as a trampoline.
It's all in bits and
that's not all,
He's burst all his
beanbags and
punctured his ball."

"Well," said Mum, "it's no surprise,
He's not getting any exercise.
We've got to think of something quick.
Can't we let him out and throw him a stick?"
"No," said Dad, "he has to hide,
He really needs to stay inside."
"Well," I said, "what about the park?
We could take him there when it's really
dark."
"No," said Dad, "he might be seen.
I've got it: let's buy him a running machine."
Our expressions made our feelings clear.
"Alright," he said, "not my best idea."

The next day quite early I went to the shed.
The two of us sat on the broken bed.
We played for a while with his brand new ball
Then sat watching a fly as it crawled up the wall.
What was that?! A loud scratching from under
the floor.
Harry walked slowly across to the door.
Before I could stop him he'd slipped outside,
Peering under the shed, his eyes opened wide.

Two eyes in the darkness were looking right
back.
He slipped straight back in and sat down for a
snack.
Eating, it seemed, always helped him to think.
He had a banana and something to drink,
Then scratching his ear with the point of his claw
He got up and boldly walked back to the door.

"What are you up to, Harry?" I said
As he pushed his two arms firmly under the shed.
Then with a creak it started to rise
And there was a cat clearly caught by surprise.
It was seized very tightly by two great big paws
And found itself staring at fearsome jaws.
And that's when I realised I'd seen her before.
It was Rosie the cat who came from next door.

The two of them looked at each other a while
Then Harry gave Rosie what looked like a smile.
He gave her a stroke and patted her head
Then putting her down he went back in his shed.
The cat had a really odd look on her face.
She sat there not moving and stared into space,
Then ever so slowly she walked to the door,
Meowed and then gave it a tap with her paw.
After a moment it opened a crack
And in walked the cat without once looking back.

And from that moment on she's come every
day.
The two of them make up games to play.
She likes to perch on Harry's head
Or snuggle up to the squidgy ted.
And Harry's a happier dinosaur,
He never breaks his things anymore.
So really there's nothing to worry about
Unless of course... Mr Riley finds out.

Chapter 4

Mr Riley's Plan

Mr Riley was not a nice man
And now he was hatching a horrible plan,
Because by chance two weeks before
He was sure he'd seen a dinosaur.
"A dinosaur? No it couldn't be,
There must be something wrong with me.
They don't exist, not anymore,
It must have been something else I saw."
He'd splashed cold water on his face
Then got his telescope out of its case.
He'd trained its lens on the open door
And there it was this time for sure.

Oh yes, he'd reported what he'd seen
For all the use that that had been.
He'd watched the policeman go into the shed
But couldn't believe what he'd come back and
said.
"Well, Mr Riley, here's the deal,
There's a dinosaur there but it isn't real."

Then everything became quite clear,
It was a truly brilliant idea.
He allowed himself a little smile
Which he hadn't done for a long, long while.
He knew that in that shed right there
Was the only dinosaur anywhere.
So first he'd catch it and take it away
And then he'd put it on display
And he'd be known for evermore
As the man who captured a dinosaur.
He'd be rich beyond his wildest dreams,
He'd be the friend of kings and queens,
He'd be in magazines and on TV shows,
Have his own jet and wear the best clothes.
And on top of that he would never more
Have to put up with those tiresome people
next door.

So he'd got himself a great big van,
A crucial part of his master plan.
And he'd lure the dinosaur into the back
By laying a trail of tasty snacks.
In the van was a cage with a lock and chain
To stop him getting out again.
But just for now he could do no more
Until no-one was at home next door.

It didn't take long for his chance to arrive.
He watched the car pulling out of the drive.
He counted the heads, one, two and three.
That was it, the whole family.
No time to lose,
He was off like a rocket
With a big bag of doughnuts wedged in his
pocket.
He climbed over the fence with the help of a chair
As the wind made a mess of his grey wispy
hair.

As he got to the shed, a noise made him freeze
And made him look up at some nearby trees.
The trees were very, very high
And from near the top he'd heard a cry.
It was very faint but a sound he knew.
"Rosie girl, is that you?"

25

He might not like this and he might not like that
But Mr Riley loved his cat.
Rosie was his only friend
And he watched as the wind caused the branches to bend.
One big gust caused her paws to slip
And then poor Rosie lost her grip.
Down and down and down she fell
With a panic stricken, piercing yell.

Mr Riley gave a shout
At the very same moment that Harry came out.
And now face to face with a dinosaur
Mr Riley passed out and fell flat on the floor.
Then Harry with a single bound
Caught Rosie before she reached the ground.

When he awoke on a broken-down bed
Mr Riley soon saw he was inside the shed
And very close by was the dinosaur
Holding Rosie gently in his paw.
Mr Riley took her and with tears of joy
Said, "You saved my Rosie, didn't you, boy?"
Then giving Harry a grateful pat
He set off with his beloved cat.

That moment he hatched a different plan
To be a better, kinder man.
So he went next door later on that night
And said, "I need to put things right.
I've been grumpy, nasty, mean and rude,
I've no excuse for my attitude.
You're going to see a better me
So here's some doughnuts for your tea,
And you, young lady, I sincerely hope
That you'll accept this gift of a telescope."

And he kept the promises he gave.
He was always ready with a smile and a
wave.
It had changed his life for evermore
Meeting Harry the hero dinosaur.

Lightning Source UK Ltd.
Milton Keynes UK
UKRC01n1148121117
312373UK00013B/47

9781788035170